by George Crenshaw

A TOM DOHERTY ASSOCIATES BOOK

This is a work of fiction. All the characters and events portrayed in this book are fictional, and any resemblance to real people or incidents is purely coincidental.

BELVEDERE
THE ODDS ARE ...

A Tor Book

Printed in the United States of America

Distributed by
Pinnacle Books, Inc.
1430 Broadway
New York, N.Y. 10018

"WHAT DO YOU MEAN, THE RUG IN THE LIVING ROOM BEGAN TO UNRAVEL SO YOU ROLLED IT UP?"

"WHY CAN'T HE JUST BURY BONES LIKE OTHER DOGS?"

"GOOD HEAVENS, IF HE WANTS TO
CLEAN OUT THE GARAGE, LET HIM."

"LOOK. I BOUGHT IT AT A DISCOUNT AND YOU HAVE A LOT
OF HEAD ROOM. NOW WHAT SEEMS TO BE THE PROBLEM?"

" ALL RIGHT!.. WHAT'S YOUR COCK AND
BULL STORY TODAY ?! "

"ONE LITTLE SPECK OF AN ISLAND IN THE PACIFIC. WHO'LL EVER FIND US?!"

"SO BELVEDERE BOTHERED YOU A LITTLE BIT. NOW, WAS THAT NICE TO DO?"

"IT'S SURE GONNA BE NICE TO GET AWAY FROM THAT PESTY POOCH FOR AWHILE"

"IF WE WERE MAKING TOO MUCH NOISE, WHY DIDN'T HE JUST COME UPSTAIRS AND SAY SO?"

"A BIT ECCENTRIC, YES, BUT IT BROUGHT A FAST HALT TO A LOT OF MYSTERIOUS SNACK-SNITCHING!"

"WHY DID YOU EVER EVEN TELL HIM ABOUT THE FLOOD OF '05?!"

"SURE IT'S CUT OUR FIRE INSURANCE IN HALF, BUT I JUST
DON'T LIKE HAVING IT WITH BELVEDERE IN THE HOUSE."

" I KEEP THINKING HOW GOOD BELVEDERE IS HAVING IT
BACK AT THE KOZY KENNELS. "

"BY JOVE, BELVEDERE WAS RIGHT. I THINK THIS *IS* KING KONG COUNTRY. "

" SO HE DOESN'T LIKE MY LEFTOVERS. DOES HE HAVE TO CALL THE FOOD AND DRUG ADMINISTRATION? "

" IF YOU'RE GOING TO MAKE SUCH A BIG THING
OF IT, I'LL GET THE PAPER MYSELF "

"SO YOU'RE WEARING YOUR NEW LICENSE AND YOU HAVEN'T
DONE ANYTHING WRONG TODAY. JUST DON'T PUSH YOUR LUCK!"

"I SUPPOSE YOU'D RATHER STILL HAVE THEM ALL
SLEEPING AT THE FOOT OF THE BED?"

"WHY DON'T YOU LEAVE YOUR BRAIN TO SCIENCE?
EVERY LITTLE BIT HELPS."

" OH, FOR HEAVEN'S SAKE, ORV. BUY HIM
ANOTHER HOT DOG. "

"MAYBE WE SHOULDN'T HAVE LEFT BELVEDERE AT HOME. HE
WOULD HAVE ENJOYED A RIGOROUS HIKE IN THE MOUNTAINS."

"WHEN ARE YOU GOING TO GET OVER THIS
FEAR OF SNAKES?"

"YOU GOT OUT TO LOOK AROUND AND THE NEXT
THING YOU KNOW **WHAT** HAPPENED?"

" I ALMOST FORGOT. THIS IS THE DAY WE DRIVE BELVEDERE
OVER FOR HIS BOOSTER SHOTS. "

" I WARNED YOU, I PLEADED WITH YOU - BUT, OH NO -
YOU HAD TO LET HIM TRY TO FIX THE PLUMBING. "

" BOY, LET'S REST AWHILE. I DON'T THINK THERE ARE ANY CROCS AROUND HERE FOR MILES. "

" CAN'T YOU TELL AN OLD CIRCUS PERFORMER WHEN YOU SEE ONE ? "

© Field Enterprises, Inc., 1979

GEORGE CRENSHAW

10-26

" IT'S EITHER AN ELECTION BET OR WE'RE LOOKING AT THE WORLD'S MOST SPOILED PET. "

© Field Enterprises, Inc., 1980

GEORGE CRENSHAW

7-2

" WHAT DO YOU MEAN, YOU THOUGHT THE BATTERY WAS 'DEAD' SO YOU BURIED IT ?! "

"BELVEDERE LIKES TO HAVE HIS DINNER PROMPTLY AT THE STROKE OF SIX."

"BELVEDERE HAS FIGURED OUT THE PERFECT SYSTEM. HE BOOKS ORV'S BETS."

"I'M SORRY I JUST HAPPENED TO CATCH A DOGFISH.
DO YOU HAVE TO TAKE IT SO PERSONALLY?"

"I'LL SAY ONE THING — HE GIVES EVERY DOG-
CATCHER A SPORTING CHANCE."

"OH, GOOD GRIEF— SO I'M CATCHING FISH WITH LITTLE HOOKS. STOP WORRYING ABOUT GOD'S RETRIBUTION."

"OH, DON'T TAKE IT SO SERIOUSLY. LOTS OF PEOPLE DON'T AGREE WITH WILLIAM BUCKLEY."

" ...AND WHAT'S MORE, HE'LL REMAIN IN THE BASEMENT
UNTIL HE'S IN A MORE REPENTANT FRAME OF MIND ! "

" YOU'RE RIGHT. THAT IS KETCHUP HE'S SHAKING
ON THE FIBULA BONE. "

" NOW IS THAT HOW I TOLD YOU TO HANG UP
MY HAT AND COAT ? "

" BELVEDERE ? WENT TO THE RACES ? GOOD HEAVENS, WHAT
WOULD A DOG KNOW ABOUT BETTING ON HORSES ? "

" SURELY THERE MUST BE SOMEONE ELSE YOU CAN GET AS A COSIGNER ? "

"IT'S A REPORT FROM BELVEDERE'S OBEDIENCE SCHOOL. IT SAYS, LORD IN HEAVEN, HAVE MERCY ON YOUR SOULS."

"ALL RIGHT, IT'S A BET. FIVE DOLLARS YOU DON'T MAKE TEN STRAIGHT BULL'S EYES."

"BY JOVE, YOU'RE RIGHT! THAT WOODPECKER IS A SURE SIGN THAT WE'RE NEAR THE PETRIFIED FOREST."

"CAN'T YOU JUST **TROT** AROUND THE NEIGHBORHOOD LIKE OTHER DOGS ?"

" ALL RIGHT. WHAT KIND OF A CRAZY CONCOCTION DID YOU DREAM UP THIS TIME ? "

"NOW THEN, ANIMAL LOVERS, YESTERDAY WE LEARNED HOW TO TELL A DOG'S AGE BY LOOKING AT HIS TEETH."

"AND WHAT'S WRONG, MAY I ASK, WITH JUST BURYING THEM IN THE GROUND?"

"ORVILLE, BELVEDERE'S BEEN WHINING AT THAT WINDOW FOR HOURS. WHY DON'T YOU LET HIM IN?"

"*GOOD GRIEF!* I'VE NEVER HEARD SUCH A FUSS OVER A LOUSY INSECT... *HERE!*"

"YOU MAY AS WELL GIVE IT UP, ORVILLE.
YOU'LL NEVER TEACH JUDO TO A DOG."

"SO WE'RE TRESPASSING IN A NEW CONSTRUCTION
AREA. WHO CARES?"

"WELL, SPEAK UP, HARGROVES, DID YOU CATCH THE WHITE SPOTTED POOCH, OR DIDN'T YOU?"

"I'M NOT AMAZED AT *ANYTHING* HE DOES!"

"SO WE HAD LOUSY LUCK TODAY.
DO YOU HAVE TO TELL THE WORLD ?!"

"NOW THAT'S WHAT I CALL A HUNGRY ANIMAL."

"IT'S HIS FOURTH HELPING, REVEREND. HE SEEMS TO BE A VERY HUNGRY OLD MAN."

"ARE YOU SURE THE WORLD IS READY FOR BUBBLE-GUM PIZZA?"

" OH, STOP COMPLAINING. HE'S GIVING YOU
A FAIR HANDICAP, ISN'T HE ? "

"HE ABSOLUTELY INSISTED ON A PENTHOUSE."

" A HUNDRED AND SEVENTEEN DOLLARS AND NINETY-FIVE CENTS FOR **WHAT** AIR CONDITIONER ? "

" WELL, WHO WON THE BIG GAME OF STRIP POKER ? "

"WHY COULDN'T HE HAVE BECOME INTERESTED IN JUST A STAMP COLLECTION INSTEAD?"

"GO RIGHT IN. HE'S EXPECTING YOU."

"WE GAVE UP YEARS AGO TRYING TO CONVINCE HIM HE WAS A DOG."

"NOW THAT'S CATERWAULING AT ITS FINEST!"

"SO I'M A FEW DAYS LATE WITH HIS ALLOWANCE. DID HE
HAVE TO TURN IT OVER TO A COLLECTION AGENCY?"

"ALL RIGHT, IN A MINUTE. I'LL BUY YOU A HAMBURGER."

"ORVILLE USES THE CROP ROTATION SYSTEM—ONE YEAR CRAB GRASS, THE NEXT YEAR WEEDS."

"HE HOPED YOU'D LIKE THEM. THEY'RE OATMEAL, SALAMI, BACON, HAMBURGER, LIVER AND RAISIN COOKIES."

" I'M SORRY, WE DON'T HAVE A MORE SCIENTIFIC NAME
FOR GARBAGE-CAN JAW. "

" SOMEHOW I THINK JEZEBEL KNOWS
WE'RE TAKING HER TO THE VETS. "

" WITH PROPER TRAINING, ANY DUMB ANIMAL CAN
BE TAUGHT TO OBEY SIMPLE COMMANDS—*COMING DEAR!*"

"YOU'RE WANTED IN THE KREMLIN."

"DO YOU HAVE A CARD FOR A DOG WHO DIDN'T TIP OVER A SINGLE GARBAGE CAN FOR A WHOLE WEEK?"

"NOW WHAT DID I SAY?"

"I'M GLAD YOU LIKED IT. IT WAS A MIXTURE OF SOWBELLY, HOGMAWS, KIDNEYS, BRAINS, GIZZARDS AND TRIPE."

"MAYBE WE NEVER SHOULD HAVE GOTTEN HIM A MOTOR BIKE."

"ALL I SAID WAS, I'M GOING TO GET A HAIRCUT."

"HEY, IT'S A COLD NIGHT. HAS ANYONE SEEN MY HOT WATER BOTTLE?"

"NEXT TIME MAYBE YOU'LL THINK TWICE BEFORE YOU CHASE A PARKED CAR."

"BEST LITTLE OL' BIRD DOG YOU EVER SAW."

"WELL, HERE WE ARE AT YOUR *SECRET* WATER HOLE. NOW WHERE ARE ALL THE WHOPPERS?"

"ALL RIGHT, ALL RIGHT! I'LL FEED YOU!"

"I SHOULD HAVE KNOWN BETTER THAN TO LET HIM FIX HIS FAMOUS DUCK SOUP."

"HE'S ORDERING WALL-TO-WALL CARPETING FOR HIS DOG HOUSE."

"CONGRATULATIONS, MADAM! THIS IS YOUR NEIGHBORHOOD PET
SHOP. YOU HAVE JUST WON A FREE PARROT AND TWO HEALTHY PUPS."

"HERE'S A GOOD BIT OF NEWS. IT'S NOT POISONOUS."

"STOP PLAYING THAT STUPID FLUTE. YOU'RE SCARING THE FISH."

"I WISH HE'D STOP SENDING AWAY FOR THINGS."

"DO YOU MIND IF WE GO FIRST? HE SWALLOWED A HAND-GRENADE."

"IT'S FATHER'S DAY, REMEMBER?"

"HIS TOY BOOMERANGS DON'T SCARE ME
ONE BIT."

"HOW'S BELVEDERE COMING WITH THE PIZZA, DEAR?"

"I THINK JEZEBEL FOUND OUT WE'VE BEEN WATERING HER MILK AGAIN."

"WHAT DO YOU MEAN, YOU FORGOT THE FILM?!"

"IT'S TIME TO HIT THE SLOPES, OLD BUDDY.
WHERE DID YOU PUT THE SKIS?"

"OUR BLOCK HAS COLLECTED $38.98. WE'D LIKE TO BUY YOUR DOG."

"ALL RIGHT, 'FESS UP. WHERE DID YOU STASH YOUR OLD BONES THIS TIME?"

"I REALIZE IT'S BEEN RAINING OUTSIDE ALL WEEK. HOWEVER..."

" I PROMISE YOU - NEXT YEAR IT'S GOING TO BE SEPARATE VACATIONS. "

" HE INSISTED ON MAG WHEELS. "

"DON'T BELIEVE THAT **VOODOO** HOKUM FOR ONE SECOND, GRIDLY. NAB HIM!"

"THIS ONE IS FOR YOU WHEN YOU SEE THE BILL."

"AMAZING! WE'RE ALL IMPRESSED. NOW LET'S GET ON WITH OUR STROLL."

"NEVER MIND. I'LL DO IT MYSELF!"

"THAT SILLY WORK BENCH OF HIS.
I WONDER WHAT HE'LL INVENT NEXT?"

"YOU AND YOUR BIRD CALLS!"

"YOU'LL HAVE TO EXCUSE BELVEDERE. HE JUST LEARNED THE WORLD TURNS FROM WEST TO EAST AND HE REFUSES TO RIDE BACKWARDS."

"IS THIS YOUR IDEA OF HELPING WITH THE YARDWORK?"

"BELVEDERE HAS HIS OWN SPECIAL WAY OF DEALING WITH PEDDLERS."

" WHAT KIND OF A CALL WAS **THAT**? "

" GOTTA RUN, MABEL. I THINK I HEARD BELVEDERE
KNOCK OVER SOMETHING. "

2-24

"ISN'T IT A LITTLE EARLY IN THE MORNING FOR TRICKS?"

7-20

"I DON'T MIND YOU CHASING CARS, BUT DO YOU ALWAYS HAVE TO GET A HUBCAP AS A SOUVENIR?"

"PERHAPS *YOU'D* BETTER MAKE MR. RHODES THE NEXT ONE, DEAR."

"IT'S THAT FRENCH POODLE UP THE STREET. DO WE KNOW ANYONE NAMED SMOOCHIE-POOCHIE?"

"HIS MASTER JUST SAID 'FINDERS KEEPERS' AND HUNG UP."

"I'VE HEARD OF BEARS TAKING FOOD FROM TOURISTS BEFORE, BUT THIS BEATS ALL!!"

"I COULDN'T FIND HIM DOWN ON THE POOP DECK EITHER."

"I WOULDN'T DRINK ANY OF HIS WEIRD COCKTAILS, DEAR. THERE MIGHT BE SIDE EFFECTS."

"WE'RE ALL TRYING TO HELP ORVILLE STOP SMOKING."

"THIS IS SCARIER THAN WATCHING THE LATE, LATE HORROR MOVIE ON TV."

"HE'S BEEN READING YOUR BOOK ON HYPNOTISM AGAIN!"

"RUN AFTER CARS IF YOU MUST, BUT WILL YOU PLEASE STOP CHASING THE GARBAGE TRUCK?!"

"IT WAS A WILD PIG HUNT."

"I SAID *ONE* LOAF OF BREAD AND A DOZEN EGGS."

"HE ABSOLUTELY REFUSES TO POSE FOR ANY PICTURE
WITHOUT A CONTRACT WITH RESIDUAL GUARANTEES."

"THEY REALLY MISS OUR LAKESIDE COTTAGE."

"ROOM SERVICE."

"HERE'S A LURE THEY CAN'T RESIST!"

"HE'S CLEANING HIS BONES *HOW?!*"

"BELVEDERE!"

"NOW THERE'S A SIGHT YOU SELDOM SEE."

"HE'S BUILDING A CONVEYOR BELT DIRECT FROM THE REFRIGERATOR."

"I STILL SAY IT CAN'T BE DONE."

"WHY COULDN'T HE HAVE BEEN SATISFIED WITH A PET GOLDFISH?"

"IF HE'D JUST BARK OR BITE, I'D KNOW HOW TO HANDLE HIM."

" NEVER MIND WHY, WHO IS YOUR NEXT OF KIN ? "

" WHAT ABOUT THE OTHER THREE RED LIGHTS YOU WENT THROUGH? "

"NO, NO, NO. NOW LET'S TRY IT ONE MORE TIME."

"BY JOVE, I THINK HE *REALLY* HAS MASTERED YOGA!"

"YOU SHOULD HAVE WATCHED WHAT HE WAS DOING!"

"YOU FORGOT THE CANDELABRA!"

"YOU GOT A NIBBLE? GOOD BOY!"

"OH, ALL RIGHT, ALL RIGHT. WHAT DID YOU DIG UP THIS TIME?"

"ALL I KNOW IS THE WINNER OF THE HOLE RIDES."

"PERHAPS YOU NEVER SHOULD HAVE MENTIONED MR. TUTTLE WORKS AT THE PACKING HOUSE, DEAR."

"THAT WHITE SPOTTED POOCH HAS DODGED ME ALL WEEK,
BUT BELIEVE ME, I'LL FIND HIM TODAY!"

© Field Enterprises, Inc., 1979

"POOR LOSER!"

"GO AHEAD, ASK ME. ASK ME IF BELVEDERE LIKED YOUR LEFT-OVER COQUILLE ST. JACQUES CAPON WITH TRUFFLE STUFFING."

"SAY, ISN'T THAT THE DOG CATCHER WE SAW CHASING BELVEDERE?"

"OH, DON'T BE SO MEAN. GIVE HIM THE EDITORIAL PAGE"

"IT'S WHAT HE WANTED FOR HIS BIRTHDAY."

"ONE WAY OR ANOTHER, BELVEDERE ALWAYS WINS."

GEORGE RENSHAW 3-10

"SO WHAT'S NEW ABOUT AIR BAGS IN CARS? I'VE BEEN DRIVING WITH TWO OF THEM FOR YEARS."

GEORGE RENSHAW

LIMEADE 5¢

LIME

2-27

"REALLY, ORVILLE, THERE MUST BE ANOTHER WAY FOR YOU TO COPE WITH BELVEDERE."

"I KNEW HE'D FIGURE OUT *SOME* WAY TO SAVE US!"

"DO WE KNOW ANYONE NAMED 'SEXPOT'?"

"WE'RE A CINCH TO CATCH HIM. HE ALWAYS HANGS AROUND THIS PACKING PLANT."

" ARE YOU TWO DUELING AGAIN ? "

" SO HE FILCHED A BONE DOWN AT THE MUSEUM. WHAT'S
ONE LITTLE OL' BONE MORE OR LESS ? "

" IT'S THE 5,000TH GARBAGE PAIL BELVEDERE RAIDED.
WE HAD IT BRONZED. "

" WHY ON EARTH DID YOU PLAY 'MELANCHOLY BABY'? "

" HE CHEWS THINGS. "

"BY THE WAY, DID YOU FEED BELVEDERE
BEFORE WE LEFT?"

" OH, GOOD HEAVENS. I FORGOT HIS AFTER DINNER BRANDY."

" ALL RIGHT, I'LL SERVE THE PIZZA ! "

"THEY'RE INSEPARABLE."

"BY JOVE, THAT'S HIS *BEST* DOGGIE TRICK ALL WEEK!"

" HE DOESN'T BITE. HE DRINKS. "

"I ALWAYS HANG MY OVERCOAT RIGHT HERE BY THE DOOR. - NOW *WHERE* IS IT??"

"WHO'S BEEN READING THIS BOOK ON VOODOO?"

"MAY I ASK JUST WHO IS TRAINING WHOM?"

"YOU HAVE TO ADMIRE HIS UNDAUNTED SPIRIT!"

"ALL RIGHT! SO I NEED A SHAVE!"

"GESUNDHEIT? IS THAT ALL YOU'VE GOT TO SAY?"

"THEY GO **ALL OUT** DURING NATIONAL DOG WEEK!"